SOUL TALK: URBAN YOUTH POETRY

A WRITING PROJECT FEATURING
SYRACUSE CITY SCHOOL DISTRICT STUDENTS

Introduction by Luis J. Rodríguez

Edited by M. Kristiina Montero

NEW CITY COMMUNITY PRESS, 2007

New City Community Press
ISBN: 978-0-9712996-8-9

Design by Angela Tsang

The mission of New City Community Press (NCCP) is to provide opportunities for local communities to represent themselves by telling their stories in their own words. We document stories of local communities because we believe their voices matter in addressing issues of national and global significance. We value these stories as a way for communities to reflect upon and analyze their own experience through literacy and oral performance. We are committed to working with communities, writers, editors and translators to develop strategies that assure these stories will be heard in the larger world.

New City Community Press
7715 Crittenden St. #222
Philadelphia, PA 19118
Phone: 315.443.1912
www.newcitypress.org

This project is supported by $3,525 in state funds, which represents .006% of the Syracuse University GEAR UP state project's total budget. This project is supported by $1,175 in federal funds, which represents .0009% of the Syracuse University GEAR UP federal project's total budget. The remaining funds ($5,550.54.1) come from Syracuse University and New City Community Press.

NCCP Publications

Working: An Anthology of Writing and Photography

Free!: Great Escapes from Slavery on the Underground Railroad

Chinatown Live(s): Oral Histories from Philadelphia's Chinatown

Espejos y Ventanas/Mirror and Windows: Oral Histories of Mexican Farmworkers and Their Families

No Restraints: An Anthology of Disability Culture in Philadelphia

Nourish Your Soul: A Community Cookbook

The Forgotten Bottom Remembered: Stories from a Philadelphia Neighborhood

Open City: A Journal of Community Arts and Culture

TABLE OF CONTENTS

ACKNOWLEDGEMENTS

This collection of writings would not have been possible without the support of many individuals. First and foremost, the following Syracuse City School District teachers who worked with the students represented in this collection should be applauded.

Rhiannon White, Corcoran High School
Marsha Zimmerman, Fowler High School
Carolyn Wolfanger, Nottingham High School
Suzanne Mayer, Blodgett Elementary School
Theresa Szpak, Clary Middle School
Danya Snihur, Grant Middle School
Roseann Esposito, Levy Middle School
Carrie O'Connor, Shea Middle School

Equally important to the success of this project were Sandy Trento, Marilyn Gray, Dr. Steve Parks, Dr. Louise Wilkinson, Dr. Susan Hynds, Carol Terry and Esther Gray for their contributions at various stages of the project and for their collective enthusiasm that helped further the project each day.

Naturally, a project of this size does not come without financial support. The following agencies helped support this project financially:

The Study Council at Syracuse University
NYSED's Extended School Day/Violence Prevention Program
School of Education, Syracuse University, Dean Douglas Biklen
Reading and Language Arts Center, Syracuse University
Professor Kathleen Hinchman

College of Arts and Sciences Writing Program, Dr. Steve Parks
Syracuse City School District, Superintendent Daniel Lowengard
GEAR UP: Gaining Early Awareness and Readiness for Undergraduate Programs at Syracuse University, Horace Smith
The University Lecture Series at Syracuse University, Michael Flusche and Esther Gray
Wegman's Food Market

FOREWORD

Art is the heart's explosion on the world. Music. Dance. Poetry. Art on cars, on walls, on our skins. There is probably no more powerful force for change in this uncertain and crisis-ridden world than young people and their art. It is the consciousness of the world breaking away from the strangle grip of an archaic social order.

~ Luis J. Rodríguez

Soul Talk: Urban Youth Poetry was born from a seemingly simple question: How can Syracuse City School District (SCSD) students be connected with Luis J. Rodríguez, award winning poet and author, and Syracuse University Lecture Series speaker? It didn't take me long to recall my positive experiences reading, interacting with, and discussing Rodríguez's memoir with first-year college students. Nearly 10 years ago, I taught in a developmental reading and study skills program at Northern Illinois University and worked with students who originated primarily from the south side of Chicago. We studied Rodríguez's memoir of gang life, *Always Running: La Vida Loca, Gang Days in L.A.*

The major writing assignment that grew out of this course was in response to Rodríguez's text. We asked students to write about a life experience in which they experienced courage and/or overcame adversity. Students wrote, rewrote, revised, and documented how they had overcome adversity and demonstrated courage. Students wrote about how they got out of gang life and into college, made difficult life decisions like choosing to have a baby or an abortion, and stopped abusing drugs and alcohol, among other personal stories. For some students, their reading and writing experiences were complemented by seeing Luis J. Rodríguez speak at a nearby college, an experience that made an impression on my students as well as on me.

I remember, on our ride back to DeKalb, IL, each of the students who accompanied me expressed that reading Rodríguez's memoir and seeing him speak so candidly about gang life, too often glamorized in the inner-city, was one of their best life experiences.

So when presented with the possibility of connecting this celebrated author and community activist with SCSD students, I jumped at the chance.

Thinking about the powerful texts written by the students from Northern Illinois University, I knew that a similar project had to be created in our Syracuse community. Together with a team of fine educators, we decided to embark on a journey of authentic writing. Our main objective became to create learning opportunities in which students participated in authentic reading and writing experiences with Rodríguez's poetry. In order for students to engage with Rodríguez's texts and the task at hand, it was crucial that they experienced the authenticity of the assignment from the beginning. The writing tasks had to be authentic—ones in which students had an intended audience and a purpose for writing that extended beyond the classroom setting while still being connected to the content. In this case, the content studied in the English classrooms was poetry, the writing task was this collection of student writing to be used in future English language arts classrooms, and the primary audience for the publication was middle and high school communities of learning.

Through a series of workshops, teachers were presented with the work of Luis J. Rodríguez and asked first to respond to the poetry as readers and then as teachers. Following these professional development sessions, the teachers presented Rodríguez's poetry to their students, mainly from his collection entitled *The Nature of Hunger*. Students were then provided with opportunities to write poetry for *Soul Talk: Urban Youth Poetry*. Some students were inspired by Rodríguez's free-verse style of writing, others were inspired by the content of his poetry, while some other students wrote about themes their souls were trying to make known to themselves and the world. In total, we received over 250 writing entries to be considered for this book. Because we didn't have space to publish all the submitted poems, our team of six educators had to make some difficult decisions.

The student-generated writing presented in this volume is accompanied by community photographs. These photographs are the result of a side-project that entailed furnishing students with disposable cameras and asking them to take photographs in response to the following prompt: "Take photographs about a day in your life without taking photographs of yourself." All photographs represented in this text are student-generated and represent how these SCSD students view their lives in their neighborhoods.

In April 2006, SCSD students carefully listened to Rodríguez read selected poems and talk about his life experiences. Close to 1000 middle school students were invited to Hendricks Chapel on the Syracuse University campus to hear the author's thoughts on the creation of community. Selected high school students had the opportunity to meet with Rodríguez in more intimate surroundings and share the poetry they had created and hear him talk about his own writing. In these intimate settings, before addressing questions about writing and poetry, Rodríguez fielded questions about gang life—entering and exiting gangs, drug and alcohol abuse, violence, faith and religion, fatherhood, and family. Rodríguez answered the students candidly.

One student asked "What about the whole gang life thing? What was that like?" Rodríguez answered: "Well, honestly, I'm going to tell you something that maybe nobody would tell you. Most of it was boring." The student audience gasped and the student who posed the question incredulously asked, "Really?" Rodríguez continued, "People think it's all exciting, that it's all, you know, fun and games. It's street life. It's nothing to do. It's hanging out, you know, you're waiting for those moments where something might happen. It's boring." The topic of conversation then moved toward writing and poetry. Rodríguez talked about writing as an outlet for anger, an outlet for one's soul to have a conversation with the world in meaningful and powerful ways instead of getting involved with violent acts. Rodríguez said, "My thing is to find a way to get that anger to come out and to find actual solutions to these things. There's no sense telling people, 'Stop being angry.' I mean, to me, that's madness. If you really have a real issue, you have to address those issues.

Now, the problem is that if you don't address them, what happens? All that anger has direction; anger has eyes. It's going somewhere. It becomes rage. And rage does not have eyes, it is blind, right? Rage lashes out everywhere. Rage is what you see in the streets, what you see when kids shoot people they don't know. It's when you see where people just can go off. It's rage.... The way to deal with rage is you have to address the issues of anger. So, I would say if you have anger you've got real issues and you've got to address them. You've got to address them in a lot of different ways before you get violent. There are so many ways. Poetry is one of the ways: writing, talking to somebody, actually resolving it, getting organized, getting the skills to know how to change things. There are a lot of ways to deal with what gets you angry. If you don't like racism, if you don't like the poor economic conditions of our communities, get the skills, organize, be a leader, and change it. That's where the real pain has to go.... Poetry and writing are one of most powerful ways to address these issues."

Rodríguez continued to talk about anger and the need for young people to find a place to express their anger without violence.
He noted:

"Poems are very important for you to find your own stories and to get close to where you think your story will take you. Living out your story is really what life is. And you may not think you have a story, you might not know that prior to the day you were born, there was no real story writing in your soul. Writing is partly finding out what that story is.... In writing I found my centering and equilibrium and I found my way home. Finding home is partly what poetry does. It gets you home. It gets you to a place where you can feel whole."

This collection of texts represents what young people in our community are feeling and thinking. They write about anger, sadness, frustration, isolation, as well as about moments of happiness and contentment in their lives in Syracuse. Some poems tell us about urban Syracuse life and some pose questions, while others attempt to offer solutions to identified problems. The students speak about their identities, families, relationships, and community. There are added voices in this collection of writing from Syracuse University students and faculty from the School of Education and The College of Arts and Sciences' Writing Program, community members who participated in Dr. Steve Parks' Syracuse community writing class, and attendees of Luis J. Rodríguez's university lecture.

All contributors wrote from their soul and they wrote with honesty. They wrote in order to find their center and equilibrium. These are their voices from the inside and the voices to which we need to listen. Within this collection, we present our collective *Soul Talk,* our inner voices.

M. Kristiina Montero, Ph.D.
Reading & Language Arts Center
Syracuse University

INTRODUCTION

LUIS J. RODRÍGUEZ

"Soul Talk" is how I describe poetry – where truth and honest emotions are conveyed through image, metaphor, and rhythm. It's a fundamental concept for anyone attempting to write or perform poetry today. Among the Mexika people of present-day Central Mexico, also known as the Aztecs, this concept was called in *tochitl, in cuicatl* – "flower and song"—the way a thinking person (*tlamatine*) or philosopher would find wisdom. Poetry, then, is one of the vital languages, one of the most important means of experiencing truth.

Unfortunately, there is a deep gulf between most language today and what is real and authentic in people. Language comes at us from all directions: TV, billboards, newspapers, magazines, the Internet, the movies. We seem to be drowning in information, often without the proper orientation to discern what is meaningful. I'd also venture to say that most of this language and information masks more than it reveals.

Can we actually trust what we read and hear? Newspapers may be about facts, but how much of this is actually truth? Politicians can turn many a strong phrase, but what they say cannot be taken at face value (most of this is called "spin"). And ads and commercials are just trying to sell you something, whether you need it or not. So where do we go to find language that is genuine, connected, and evoking?

I would look toward poetry, which has been making an upsurge over the past thirty years. Much of this is linked to the rise of Rap, a contemporary re-working of the griot tradition, a healing language art mostly created by youth with little economic or social resources – and not much schooling either. Although the music industry has captured and corrupted much of the profitable end of this art (as they've done with music, painting, theater, and the mass media), the essence remains: free expression, imagination, and storytelling.

Since the mid-1980s, we've seen the growth of the Poetry Slam or poetry performance scenes. While its roots are in 1950s Beat Poetry, L.A. Stand Up Poetry, Black Poetic Expression (the Last Poets and the Watts Prophets), New York's Nuyorican Café, and Chicano/Native/Women/Gay voices, a major source originated from de-industrialized Chicago, where local poets combined competition and language/story into an exciting mix of words and delivery – poetry to be experienced.

And we can't forget the free-wheeling expansive poetry, much of it academic, that Americans have been writing for more than 150 years (often in contrast to the older, stodgier, British traditions) – from Walt Whitman to Emily Dickinson, Ezra Pound to Sylvia Plath, Allen Ginsburg and beyond (including contemporary writers like Billy Collins, Joy Harjo, Terrance Hayes, Sherman Alexie, Jack Grape, and Sandra Cisneros).

Today I visit hundreds of schools throughout the country. I've noticed an exciting upsurge in poetry classes, poetry cafes, and author readings – thanks to innovative teachers and school administrators. I've also seen how many young people carry their own journals or keep their own computer files with work they've done for themselves – not for an assignment or a grade. Something in us knows that we have to move toward deep and meaningful language, that we have to reclaim and re-invigorate the word.

The anthology *–Soul Talk: Urban Youth Poetry* – that you hold in your hands is a substantial contribution to what "soul talk" is about: voices, ideas, experiences, sentiments, flowers, and songs. Please read these works as anyone would read any good poetic expression – over and over again, to savor more than once, and to discover new details, images, and layers of meaning.

— Luis J. Rodríguez, written in Mexico City, October 12, 2006

A WRITING PROJECT FEATURING
SYRACUSE CITY SCHOOL DISTRICT STUDENTS

EYE TO EYE

Akua A. Goodrich

You see me on the street and you don't even speak, not even a smile or simple Hello!
Yet, you say the thought of me dying makes your heart weak.
Time Will Tell.

Are you so scared, so full of fear? Oh' you don't wanna go there...
I'm not askin' you to put yo' life on the line... Just show me that you care.

Do, I care? Yeah, I care about mine. About me and my community...
Through all the bloodshed and poverty...it's Love that sets me free.
Everything you've seen or read you can not believe...
From the tales of self-hatred to the abuse I've received.
Oh, Time Will Tell.

My eyes sing and my heart screams...
Come and share your dreams with me, so I can see...
I have two sets of eyes...is what my mother told me.
See...That's Love. I'm Talkin' real love.

No, Uh Uh, now come on, I'm not asking for your sympathy...just for you
to share with me your vision of life and how you overcame adversity.

Lord, pleeeease have mercy on my soul. I don't think I can take no more...
Of the duckin' and dodgin' still I gotta remain strong!
How about you?
Time Will Tell.

I may not display strength, as you know it or strength as you show it,
or strength as you live it or as you give it...But it's what I have.
I've been told that I am brilliant, beautiful, handsome and talented...
that my creativity and social skills are that of a true leader.
But, what do you think about me?
Time Will Tell.

See I really want to get to know you and maybe love you - like Family.
I want you to share your knowledge and wisdom with me and I with you.
Isn't that what they call RECIPROCITY.
Time Will Tell.

It may take some time, some time for me to unwind, for me to smile, to let you in.
But, when and where do we begin?
May I suggest you use those inner eyes to seek and find?
"Cause, I have two sets of eyes...is what my mother told me.
See...That's Love. I'm talkin' real Love.

Akua is a writer, poet, and motivational speaker whose purpose in life is to "empower individuals to empower each other." Since 1996, Akua and her husband Anthony have served over 3,000 young people through the Syracuse, New York-based Power Unit for Motivating Youth (PUMY) organization.

A TATTOO'S STORY

BY JAKK G. III

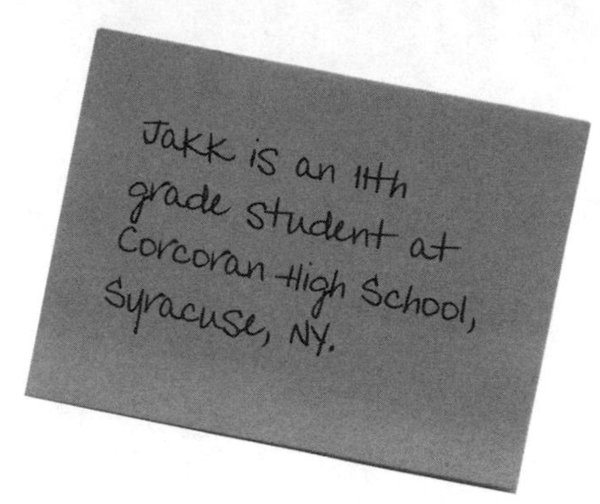

I have a tattoo and it tells a story.
My tattoo says "Jakk" with two k's
You're supposed to spell it with a "ck," but not me
That's how my father spells it
And how my grandfather spells it
My grandfather is an old, mean, selfish drunk
I don't see any of him in me
Not one bit
My father also spells it with a "ck"
But once again, not me
My father is a dead-beat dad
A drunk, a drug addict, abusive, a liar and much more
So I don't see any of him in me either
That's why I spell my name differently
The only thing I got from my father
Is my physical strength
Everything else comes from my mother
Maybe I should change my name to Brenda
Like my mom

ANGEL EYEZ

Ebony Stewart

A pair of soft brown eyez gazed upon me as soon as I entered this world.
He whispered in my ear, "You're Daddy's baby girl."
He took me in his broad arms and cradled me.
He looked me in my eyez and promised he'd never leave.

One year later, "DaDa" was the words I would say.
I waddled around the house looking for the angel eyez
that cradled me that day.
I searched the closet, the hamper and the den.
I even searched the bin which my toys were in.

"MaMa, where's DaDa?" I began to whine.
Then I asked Grandma and Grandpa and so on down the line.
No one knew or there was something they weren't telling me.
In my head, I was daddy's baby girl and would always be.

I found my "DaDa" ten years later when his family and he were sitting
by a tree.
I remember when I was born; he told me he would never leave.
So, I looked at him and whispered goodbye to those big brown angel eyez.

Photo credit: Corey Pringle

*Corey is an 11th grade student at Fowler High School. His favorite activities are driving around, hanging out with his friends, and completing homework. He wants others to view him as a friendly and kind person.

Ebony is an 11th grade student at Corcoran High School, Syracuse, NY.

Photo credit: Alfredo Del Moral

*Alfredo is a 12th grade student at Fowler High School. His favorite pastimes are volleyball and photography. Friends and family are important to him, but he doesn't let them control his life entirely.

ALONE IN THE DARK

Charles Johnson

I lay on the bed in the
Dark and I think,
Where do I belong?
I feel isolated from the world,
No one understands me.
The comments, the stares,
The ridicule. Is this what
My life consists of?
I try to fit in, but I don't
Belong anywhere.

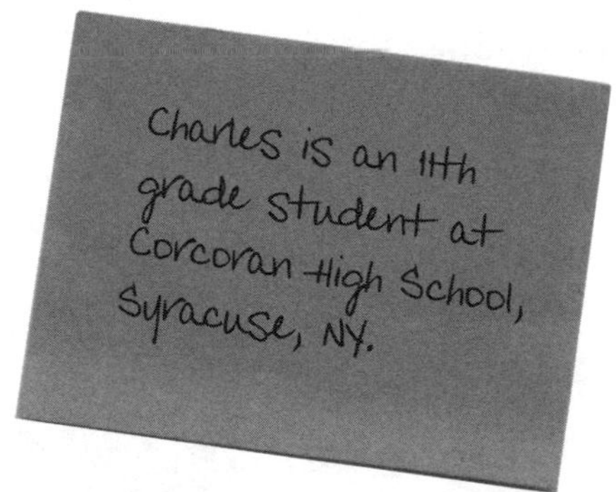

ANGER

Joan DeArtemis

Anger is . . .
My constant companion
My loyal friend who sits at my
Feet and chews on rawhide while
I write stories on my computer.

My rage sleeps with me at night
And wakes me up when I feel threatened
No one can know me for long
Before they know about my anger friend

People usually accept that about me
They know I control my rage
Keep it on a leash,
And clean up its messes
When I've gone

But you know what?
I'm not apologetic
Where I go, my anger goes with me
As my mother would say,
"Love me, love my dog."

Joan is a student at Syracuse University. She is pursuing a minor in the writing program.

Photo credit: Alessia Curle

*Alessia is a 10th grade student at Fowler High School. She enjoys being around her friends at school and her family. Her friends and family help her enjoy life.

RAINY DAY

Roxanne Bocyck

The rain is falling, washing away
My negative days
My negative thoughts
It is a warm rain
Showers of hope
The raindrops say,
"Life is worth living,
Life is worth all the troubles
That may come your way."
So don't despair
About the rain
It cleanses the soul
And makes you smile
Again.

MY RACE IS NOT TROUBLE

Cherelle Pace

My skin is black
And because of that
They treat me like I'm trouble
I'm really nice
And I don't bite
I'm hard-working and I'm humble
I'm not a slave
So don't portray
That I've worked on plantations
So give me respect.
For I have success
Because I have dedication
What my ancestors did
Was placed in my skin
Now I am stereotyped
I will not give up
No matter what
I will win this constant fight!

*Cherelle is an 8th grade student at Shea Middle School in Syracuse, NY. She plans on attending college to become a landscape architect.

WHY I WRITE

BY BRANDICE BELL

WHY DO I WRITE? FOR A PERSON LIKE ME WHO IS NEVER SHORT ON WORDS, ONE WOULD THINK THAT WOULD BE AN EASY QUESTION TO ANSWER. However, I seem to be finding it quite difficult to respond, seeing as how thirty minutes after starting this composition all I have written is "Why I Write." To me, writing is not just a means of expression; it is also a means of repression. To take words out of my complex, worry-filled mind and to place them on paper is my way of maintaining my sanity.

Growing up, I had four brothers and sisters ranging from nine years younger than me to seven years older than me. My house was rarely empty and I'd steal opportunities to be home alone every chance I got, despite my mother's concern, until I was about thirteen. Amidst all of the noise and confusion, I found myself very lonely most of the time and I often resorted to talking to myself. I had friends and my siblings were cool, but I found the easiest and most natural way to clear my head was to talk to myself. I still do today, but now my rantings have evolved into writing. I write when I am angry and I write when I haven't a care in the world. It allows me to separate myself from my body and peer into the looking glass of my heart. I write to understand myself better, and also in the hope that others will too.

There are thousands of words in the English language and in other languages as well, but writing is so empowering to me because the writer has the ability to create a collection of those words that have been used in various ways by various people and make them his or her own. My father used to say to me, "You may have money, friends, and power, but at the end of the day, your word is all you have." I've always thought that this piece of advice was a parable on keeping your promises, but now I realize that the statement can be taken literally. A person's word is all they have. Those that harbor their thoughts deep within themselves and who don't allow people to see their true selves really have no power at all. To speak is to give conviction to your thoughts and to write is to make those thoughts concrete, even if only in your mind. I never write in pencil or erasable pen—not because I never make mistakes, but because I enjoy the process of writing, mistakes and all. Sometimes it's in the mistakes that I have scratched out or written above that I find the most inspiration.

My writing allows me to connect to the past through my own eyes. Rereading things that I have written, whether it be a poem or song, a research paper, or even a grocery or to-do list, sends me on a journey into a part of me that I may have forgotten or never knew existed. Writing acts as my anchor in the turbulent seas of worldly existence. It grounds me and forms the foundation to ensure my stability while still tolerating and contributing to my growth.

I think everyone is a writer, whether they know it or not. You don't need a degree or license to write, you just need to feel. For this, writing may arguably be one of the least discriminating jobs in existence. So, why do I write? Because I can.

*Brandice is a student at Syracuse university. She is pursuing a minor in the writing Program.

Photo credit: Alessia Curle

POWER

Anonymous

Community is people coming together for a purpose of good,
Regardless of color, race, religion, or gender.
Change has to come from the heart, the mind will follow.
Art can communicate.
Communication is power.
Power can change.

CREATING COMMUNITY

Anonymous

Creating community can be achieved
if people weren't afraid
to talk to one another,
to get to know each other.

JUST BECAUSE

Ebony Stewart

Just because I don't talk,
Doesn't mean I have nothing to say.
Just because I don't go to church,
Doesn't mean I don't pray.
Just because I'm quiet,
Doesn't mean I won't get loud.
Just because I made a few mistakes in my life,
Doesn't mean I'm not proud.
Just because I don't fight,
Doesn't mean I can't thump.
Just because I'm not easily provoked,
Doesn't mean I won't jump.
Just because I know myself,
Doesn't mean I'm found.
Just because I appear alone,
Doesn't mean my friends aren't around.
Just because I go to school every single day,
Doesn't mean I'm the goody two-shoes that ya'll say.
Yeah, this is me and unlike most,
I can admit my reality:
I don't know who I am,
But I know who I want to be.

Photo credit: Alessia Curle

WHAT IS WRONG WITH YOUR CREATION?

BY RAKEA WEAKFALL

What is wrong with me?
Am I too dark or maybe too light?
Is it the fact that I may roll my tongue,
Or maybe get violent when I see a gun
Is it 'cause I'm sweet and not the other way around?
Did you expect for me to fail,
And later come pay a
Five hundred dollar bail?
What is wrong with me?
Is it that I think before I proceed
Rather than stumble like the rest
Of your children?
But they still end up on their feet.
Or hey, is it that
I just wanted to be with you?
To have that love
Yeah, that love that I'm now feignin' for
Like a bottle of NQ, that love that is now forever gone
"Why?" you ask. Well, I'll let you answer that one
As I said, "What is wrong with me?"
Please tell me 'cause I'm so
Damn tired of trying to please.

A SEED IS PLANTED

Joanne O'Toole

A humble seed
falls to the fertile ground.
No one sees it.
No one notices.
But there it lies
hoping.

A soft raindrop
falls from the sky.
Bathing the seed,
giving it promise.

The warm sun
emerges from the clouds.
Blanketing the seed,
giving it promise.

A single child
walks to a worn desk.
No one sees him.
No one notices.
There he sits
hoping.

A wise teacher
approaches the child
seeing in him
unrevealed promise.

The capable teacher
feeds his student's
mind and soul
revealing his promise.

A tattered humanity
seeks to become one.
Everyone sees it.
Everyone notices.
There it waits
hoping.

A compassionate person
reaches out to a stranger
extending a hand,
imagining the promise.

Impassioned neighbors
come together
heart and soul,
realizing the promise.

UNA SEMILLA SE PLANTA

Una semilla humilde
Cae a la tierra fértil.
Nadie la ve.
Nadie la siente.
Pero allí yace
En esperanza.

Una gota suave
Cae del cielo
Bañando a la semilla,
Dándole posibilidades.

El sol caluroso
Sale de las nubes
Abrigando a la semilla,
Dándole posibilidades.

Un niño solitario
Camina al pupitre gastado.
Nadie lo ve.
Nadie lo siente.
Allí se sienta
En esperanza.

Un maestro sabio
Se le acerca al niño
Viendo en él
Incontables posibilidades.

El maestro hábil
le alimenta al niño
El espíritu y la mente
Descubriendo adentro sus posibilidades.

Un mundo roto
Busca armonía.
Todos lo ven.
Todos lo sienten.
Allí queda
En esperanza.

Una persona compasiva
Se extiende al ajeno
Ofreciendo una mano,
Imaginando las posibilidades

Vecinos apasionados
Se inspiran a unirse de
alma y corazón,
Realizando las posibilidades.

*Joanne is a doctoral student in the School of Education at Syracuse university. She is a former high school Spanish teacher and is the president-elect (2006) of the New York State Association of Foreign Language Teachers.

My NAME ISN'T BILLY'S LITTLE SISTER

Cherelle Pace

My name isn't Billy's little sister.
My name is not Twin.
My name is Cherelle, sometimes called evil.
I'm honest and stubborn and sharp as a needle.
My name is from the great Indian culture.
My name represents my fashion couture.
My name isn't rude, 'cause that's just not me.
I'm tired of people calling me mean.
My name means justice and things that are right.
My name means brains and things that I might.
My name isn't nerd because I multi-task.
My name is Cherelle, with words
Causing heart attacks.

MY NAME IS NOT SANTA

Jonathan Santa

My name is not Santa
My name is Santa (pronounced "Sunta").
My name came from a strong family.
My name came from someone special.
My name is like Santa Clause.
I hate my name.
People are always talking about it.
People treat me like I am the real
Santa
I tell them that I am not the real Santa
I am Santa (pronounced "Sunta").

Jonathan is an 8th grade student at Shea Middle School. He was born and raised in Syracuse, NY. Jonathan's goal is to become a professional baseball player or a criminal investigator.

SHUT UP

Ashley Barclay

If you mean it
Then say it
If not
Shut your mouth
'Cause anything that comes out of
Your mouth
Doesn't matter one bit
You gossip
You speak
What you don't know
And when you're told so
The words keep flowing out
The lies keep coming
They never stop
And you never learn your lesson.

MISTAKES

Ashley Barclay

Mistakes
Are parts of everyday life
To ignore them would be impossible
But I strive
To reach for that eraser
Only to find
In life
In reality
Truly
There are none

Ashley is an 8th grade student at Levy Middle School. She enjoys reading and plays. When she enters high school she hopes to join the drama club.

WHY I WRITE
BY MINNIE BRUCE PRATT

A LONG WALK THROUGH THE WORLD

WHEN I WAS 11 OR 12, SOMEONE GAVE ME A PINK LEATHERETTE DIARY. My handwriting was big and loopy, and the space allotted for each day—four lines—was too small. Even if I had shrunk my words down to a tiny size, the space was too small. I tried to write in it anyway, but there was no room to think.

When I was 12 or 13, I went into my mother and father's bedroom, looking for something, I didn't know what, some answer to why we lived the way we did. Some answer to my father's drinking, my mother's tight angry face, some answer. I pulled open the drawers of their fake mahogany dresser, and in the third drawer down, under my mother's folded slips and bras, there was a diary, her diary from the early years of her marriage. I opened it and read some of the pages, which answered nothing, which told me only that she had no answers. I put the diary back. She saw that I had been in her things, though she never said a word to me. But later I saw her out by the garage, dropping some burning object into the wire trash basket. Later, when I looked again in the dresser drawer, the diary was gone.

When I was 12 or 13, I started keeping a journal in spiral-bound notebooks. The pages were lined, but unlimited in number. When I got to the end of one book, I bought another, and kept writing. Sometimes I go back to those journals today and read my words, and I am sad and embarrassed. I hear the voice of a girl talking to herself and lying. She writes to prove herself to an invisible presence, as if to someone who is always listening as she fills page after page with the small events of her daily life. She is talking not to her mama leaning over her shoulder, but to God. She is lying without even knowing she is lying. She describes her actions every day to show how she has kept the world orderly by doing what is expected of her. Over and over she proves that she is a good girl. She doesn't ask questions about her life. She doesn't wonder if perhaps God would like her to ask questions rather than write out the same answers over and over.

Since I was 12 or 13, I have kept a journal, except for a few years when I entered college, got married, and had two babies. Those were the years I didn't write but lived out the answers I'd put down earlier, how to have a home, how to have a husband, how to have a family. Nothing about how to have a self—that would be "selfish," the opposite of being good, in a woman. I started keeping my journal again after being in conversations with women who were part of early women's liberation; they kept asking me questions. When I look back at those begun-again pages, my handwriting slopes and falls across the paper. I sprawl, I ignore the lines. It is the writing of a mad woman, incoherent, distraught, furious, shouting questions at herself: What is love? What is home? What is my work in the world?

Since I was 12 or 13, I have kept a journal, for almost 40 years. During those years, I have had many homes, and only one, the work of my writing. I practice in my journal every day, and the exercise is: How do I talk to myself without lying? How do I tell myself more than one truth? Now I write on a computer, not in notebooks, but I still print out every page. The pages laid end to end would be a long walk through the world.

*Minnie is a professor at Syracuse university in the writing Program and in women's Studies.

IF ONLY

Katheryn Costello

If only I could crawl out of my own skin,
for just one day.
To analyze some of the hurtful things that I sometimes
do or say.
I sit here, unhappy with who I've become,
looking perfectly happy and carefree to some.
I wonder if it's possible to change
the way that has been paved for me.
But at times I feel that I should just let it be.
For I have a guard up,
one that has been there for so long.
Sometimes it's able to protect me
when someone does me wrong.
But it's not fair for others
who care for me as best as they can,
who were there for me when things got tough,
who were there for me when I ran.
Running is the only sensible thing that I've done lately
other than keeping my mouth shut.
I just don't know anymore.
I always seem to be in a rut.
All of my energy was wasted throughout two years.
I'll gain it back somehow.
All I can do is my best,
and live for now.

*Photo credit: Alfredo Del Moral

"FOWLER VS. THE MEDIA"

Alfredo Del Moral

With a clear view of Geddes Street
rest some bricks that are not quite right,
and the traces of mud on feet
offer such a horrid sight.
So completely struck with ignorance,
what a dreadful place to be.
Lacking any welcoming acceptance,
can this be anyone's cup of tea?

We are not to be taken seriously,
for our learning goes in vain.
We poor, poor Fowler students
go through such unbearable pain.
We will never go to college,
and wear that shameful pointy hat
because our futures will only consist of
"do you want fries with that?"

You may think this is how I feel
but shattering your thoughts, I do enjoy,
proving this school's "rep" isn't made of steel.

As the blatant are hushed and made coy
for the eyes rather than for the ears
of those who see Fowler surrounded
by bullets, drowning in its tears.
Was that the intention of this school when founded?

Our mouths are carefully stitched shut by a
hand holding a whip and shackles.
Protecting a virgin who is already a prostitute
to all who hear mother hen's cackles.
It is useless to ask why a student fails
to participate or maintain a high average,
when the importance is put into the sales
of our poor school's media carnage.

*Photo credit: Brandon Irving

Brandon is a 12th grade student at Fowler High School. He is an aspiring actor, director, author, poet, and artist. He would like to major in art and literature in college.

TRUTH AS IS

Kwiree Keene

Lost in the crowded streets of life
rejection is the terrible
end. And acceptance is the name
of the game. But so few of us
make the grade.

Half dressed is the style
this decade, but it's not me. There
are some who claim individuality
but you're not, it's just another
form of acceptance.

Is there a cool group or are we
all a bunch of lames? Does anyone
accept us or do we all just reject? Do
we speak just to talk or do
we speak to be heard? Everyone
thinks they know the game,
but no one really knows how to play it.

Don't criticize my words
or tweak my story. Because deep
down inside you know it's the
truth as is.

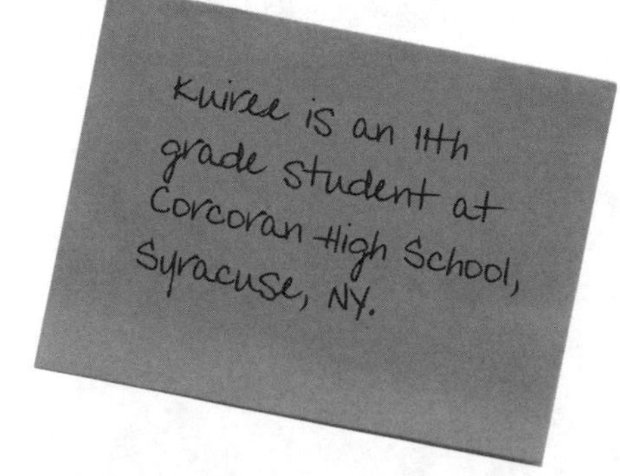

WHY DOES IT STILL HAPPEN?

Alen Jusic

Why do our classmates drop out of school
When they know education is the best way to succeed?

Why do our friends kill each other
When we all can help prevent that?

Why does our country go to war
When war is the darkest piece of a solution?

Why do we want to be different from each other
When we are all the same in front of God?

Why are things the way they are
When we can make the world a better place?

*Alen is a junior at Nottingham High School. He moved to Syracuse, NY in 2001 from his native Bosnia. He is 17 years old.

MY GENERATION

Aubrey Hall

People always talking crap,
They just wanna get slapped,
They always say we are the bad ones,
They are the ones that give us little or none.

We try our best to succeed in life,
They're the ones that put us down like a puncture
In the heart with a knife.
They think of us as being dumb
But they are a bunch of nobodies.

Life is already very hard in the new millennium.
Putting us down and criticizing us is doing
The minimum.
Why treat us this way?
When they get old
They're going to need us one day.

My generation is powerful,
We might not all get along.
They can keep criticizing,
But we're growing strong.

*Photo credit: Alessia Curle

Aubrey is an 11th grade student at Corcoran High School, Syracuse, NY.

BROTHER WAS A SOLDIER

Lindsy Lee

Brother was a soldier,
He taught me about freedom.

I am getting pressured into a gang,
It's hard.

Brother said, "It is your choice and your decision."

This is my freedom.
This is my war.
I am at war.

Lindsy is a 14-year-old 8th grade student at Grant Middle School, Syracuse, NY. She is interested in film and has a passion for writing stories, poems, and songs. In the future, Lindsy hopes to combine her writing and interest in movies to write scripts and create films.

THE TRI-FOLD FLAG

George Smith

Dedicated to my father, Wilford M. Smith

The tri-fold flag—for what does it stand?
For sacrifice in a foreign land
For shivering in below zero cold and sweating in 100-plus heat
For an enemy that is also suffering they will meet
They face bullets and bombs
Some go home
Over others they read a psalm
This flag here, you see,
Has very special meaning to me
It belonged to my dad
He came home and I am a son he had
He told me of the horrors of war
He drank so he would not remember them anymore
He was among the first to enter Dachau—a living hell
It gave him nightmares; he was never well
The medals he received he tossed in a roadside brook
He said no to a medal for saving five lives the war almost took
He said nobody ever wins at war
The number of dead is how they keep score
When you see a flag-draped coffin please try to see
If it was not for someone's sacrifice
Would there be a you or me?

*George lives in Syracuse, NY.

OUR CHILDREN

Rhiannon White

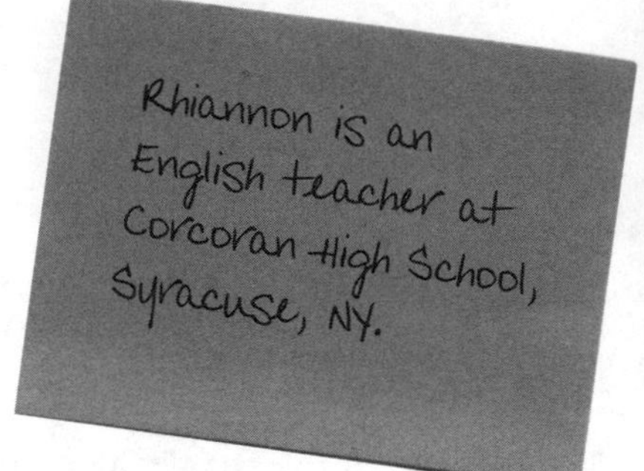

If bullets whiz
and sirens roar,
what do we think
our children live for?

If children have to run
and hide to cry,
why do you think
they fight, steal and lie?

If they continue to wish
but have nothing solid to hold,
why do you think,
they don't do what they're told?

If every turn and every corner
leads to a dead end,
how do we think
these hearts we can mend?

If each and every day
ends with a cold and hungry night,
why do you think
our children can't think, read and write?

If they never believe
that they can reach the sky
All the years will come and go
and surely pass them by

If we stop wondering why
and teach our children to love and to try
If we spread their wings and give them a way to fly
they will stop killing and choosing to die

WHY I WRITE

BY DIANNA WINSLOW

WHY DO I WRITE? I WRITE TO UNDERSTAND WHAT MY BODY FEELS AND KNOWS. SOMETIMES WHAT I END UP KNOWING SURPRISES ME WHEN IT COMES OUT OF MY FINGERS AND ONTO THE COMPUTER SCREEN. IT CAN BE ABOUT ANYTHING: WORK I'M THINKING ABOUT PROFESSIONALLY OR FAMILY AND RELATIONSHIPS I AM INVOLVED IN OR A CIVIC PROJECT I'M TRYING TO UNDERSTAND. OR WHY I AM DRAWN TO A RECIPE I KNOW AND CAN'T FIGURE OUT HOW TO TELL MY SON HOW TO COOK—YOU KNOW, WHATEVER COMES UP IN ANY PART OF MY LIFE.

*Dianna is a graduate student in the writing Program at Syracuse university.

STREETS

Janice Mendez

Streets
Dangerous, Scary
Gangs, Criminals, Jail
Drug addictions, Blood
No return

*Janice is a 7th grade student at Blodgett Middle School. She is of Puerto Rican descent.

STREETS

Ardel Joe

Fire at my feet
Girlz all 'round
Don't cross the yellow tape
Homicides in town
Where ambulances stay drivin' by
All year round

*Ardel is a student at Levy Middle School, Syracuse, NY.

URBAN LIFE

Charae Standard

I hear the cries of the street
The wind speaks of heartache and despair
The trees grow no more and the flowers disappear
The sun has lost its shine
And the sky is no longer blue
A concrete jungle filled with violence and hate
Is that all that is left for you?
The sounds of the owls are drowned out by sirens,
The chirps of crickets turn into mothers crying
Take a deep breath and let the cold air freeze your heart
As this harsh urban life does right from the start

Photo credit: Courtney M. Raeford

Photo credit: Brandon Irving

Photo credit: Jodeann Harris

Jodeann is a 10th grade student at Fowler High School. Her favorite activities are dancing, singing, playing volleyball, and listening to music. She dreams of becoming a pediatrician.

WORKING CLASS BLUES

Linda Campbell

God, country, family, friends
Where are we when jobs come to an end?
We work hard all our lives for work and pay
When jobs disappear, who among us can say
Dreams evaporate as though never there
Homes foreclosed as we sit and stare
No sense of worth
No job! No job!
No sense of self
Where is God?
Who will take care of our family that we pledged and sweated to do?
Who will take care of us when we're scared through and through
I hear this same cry in any number of ways
Many workers who count and count the days
Uncertainty has taken a weighty toll
No work! No welfare! No charity dole!
We'll make it, we say, how can we not
We come from the working class, how can we stop.
No sense of worth
No job! No job!
No sense of self
Where is God?
I know my God!
I will find a job!

*Linda Campbell lives in Syracuse, NY.

SCARED

BY JENNIFER DITCH

Every day I walk in fear
watching people standing near.
Having to watch them is a scary thought,
listening to them talk and talk.
Police cars are always near,
letting us know not to be in fear.
When someone is wearing red,
either there's a fight going to happen or someone is dead.
Not being able to play outside,
means someone is not alive.
Living in my neighborhood is like watching a war,
that is when we shut the doors.
Every night I go to bed,
listening to people in dread.
Hearing gunshots every night,
makes people jump in fright.
Having to wake up to screams,
makes me scared to even dream.
Every night they wait for us to go inside,
that is when they start the crime.

*Jennifer is a 10th grade student at Fowler High School. Her favorite hobbies include skateboarding, soccer, volleyball, hanging out with friends and family, listening to rock music, and watching scary movies.

BEHAVIORAL SINK

Angelica Chapman

The block you call yours
Was once owned by distinguished individuals.
With no one to claim their inheritance
But cyclic deterioration.
Now to be rented out by drop-outs and whores,
The landlords profit in the modem hierarchy.

Diversity isn't so great when everything becomes the same.
The beginning is like a new revolution
And the end is only the beginning.
The church calls it the work of the devil.
Although sometimes it feels that way.

This is the true definition
Of moral degradation.
Where we suffer from lethal dosages of an increasing population.

This country promised us something long ago.
But our endless cries remain unheard.
This was supposed to be our refuge.
A place for freedom and safety.
Yet in return, we were cast away by the law.
Only to be questioned about our American citizenship.
Here, in the city
Blacks, Whites, Hispanics, Asians, Muslims, Heterosexual/Homosexual
They are all equally worthless.

Photo credit: Brandon Irving

Angelica is a senior at Fowler High School. She is always ready for a good debate. She is political, analytical, open-minded, and, don't forget, exuberant.

WE HAD MUSIC

Alice Mihigo

Children were crying loudly
There was blood all over the clouds.

But our land was taken;
We didn't have food.

But still our hearts were filled with goodness
Because we had music.

We danced all night
And, yes, we did all right.

Because we had music,
Some of us were dying with a big smile,
with music.

LISTEN

Brandon Irving

Listen to the discordant lullaby
Of children's laughter muffled by
Traffic and shrieking sirens of the ambivalent ambulance cry

Observe the stuttering litter dancing around
The urban guerrillas who loiter
On the cracked concrete street corner
Dispensing death to the misguided youth

Feel the restricting frostbite cold hold
Of the chainlink barriers binding the mind
By the habitual ritual of the nine to five
Imprisoned behind the bars of the minimum wage cage
Barely sufficient to survive

Realize it is more than possible to thrive on the bare necessities
Once you have become a victim of the catastrophe of success
Probability has it that you may forget where you are from
So keep it in mind that you are what you have endured and that
What doesn't kill you will only make you stronger

A COMMUNITY IN MOURNING

Helen Hudson

It is another dreary day in the city of Syracuse; it is a day that is full of dread, for this is the day that we will bury another of our young. This is a scene that has been playing out in our communities for too long. We are not supposed to bury our children—they are supposed to bury us. Our young doctors, our young lawyers, hell, even our next president. And they are dying at the hands of one another. Our young have no hope. Our young feel that there is no love. But they are wrong—they are very loved. I think they fail to realize that they are our future, our future dreams. They are what our elders fought and gave their lives for, so that in the future their great-great-great grandchildren would have a better life than they did. Granted, there has been some progress over the years, but there is still so far to go. Our communities need to become just that—communities. Communities like the one from my era, which wasn't too long ago, when neighbors looked out for the neighbors and when your child did something wrong you knew it before they hit the door. When you could watch kids run up and down the streets and gunfire did not rain on their heads; when the Fourth of July meant celebrating our independence and not showing our dependency to all the evils that the world has to offer. When our young saw the struggles that we endured, when we banded together and showed our strength in numbers. Now the strength is shown with guns. Our children are dying. Where there were community centers and bandwagons, now there are boarded-up buildings and the hopelessness of a generation that feels so lost. It is up to us, the Sojourner Truths and the Frederick Douglass's of the world: our children are dying and it is our duty, as it was for our spirits of the past, to stand fast and come to the rescue of our children. Here we are as a community gathering again to bury one of our young—a young man who will never be a husband, or a father to his children, or a son to his mother, or a friend to a friend because our children are dying. And it just breaks my heart.

*Helen lives in Syracuse, NY.

*Photo credit: Alessia Curle

Photo credit: Brandon Irving

John is a 12th grade student at Fowler High School. He enjoys reading, writing, and playing soccer. He has wanted to be a police officer since he was two years old. He wants to major in criminal justice in college.

WILL YOU CLEAN THIS UP?

John Forrester

Broken dreams and pieces of garbage
Litter the street
Old food containers and beer bottles
Are the décor
Why won't someone clean this up?

Babies having babies and single branches
Of the family tree
Hustling and stealing just to survive
Is stealing stealing if it's for a life?
Why can't someone clean this up?

You grow up and move out
And move to a better part of town
Never looking back, not even to reminisce
About how nice it was when you lived here
And how bad it's gotten since
Why won't you clean this up?

WHY I WRITE

BY DAVID A. NENTWICK

I WRITE TO STAY IN CLOSE TOUCH WITH PEOPLE FAR AWAY.
I WRITE TO LET PEOPLE KNOW WHAT'S ON MY MIND.
I WRITE TO PARTICIPATE ACTIVELY AS A MEMBER OF MY COMMUNITY.
I WRITE SO THAT I CAN TRY TO FIGURE SOMETHING OUT.
I WRITE TO EXPERIENCE THE SHEER JOY OF WORD PLAY.
I WRITE TO GET THINGS DONE.

*David is a doctoral student in the writing Program at Syracuse university.

Kevin is an 8th grade student at Levy Middle School. He loves the Spice Girls and enjoys drawing.

UNITY AND FORGIVENESS

Anonymous

These two words must go hand in hand. Without one, the other fails. As both are mutually cultivated, the development of our society will grow. Without them, our communities will slowly self-destruct from the inside out. As bitterness and revenge take their stronghold on today's youth, the next generation that our society will face will be one of separation.

We will have recessed the work of our ancestors over the past 150 years. The very struggle that our ancestors fought for will present its ugly truth.

LIKE IT OR NOT

Kevin Mulder

I like singing
I like art
I like dancing
But I don't like basketball.

MOTIVATION

Cassandra Neuser

Shattered dreams
and broken lives.
Children armed
with guns and knives.

Drug dealers standing on the corner
looking for a sale.
Desperate people do desperate things
and then they end up in jail.

This city life can consume you
if you let it get you down.
And when you're in need the most,
no one will be around.

But if you keep your head up
and stay focused on your dreams
Escaping this chaotic city life
is all the motivation you need.

I KID

Michael Touron

I joke, it's the ghetto, I kid, it's the slums
But it's not as bad as many think when they come.
Not the cleanest, I know, nor the quietest around.
And there's a lot of holes in the ground.
But I call it home and I call it the ghetto.

My neighbor's job is enigmatic. Who knows what he does?
Mom joshes that he's a crack dealer
Why else would people visit at all hours of the night?
He was shot in the leg due to a "disagreement," according to the news.
We think he gave a bad batch, and we know it's the ghetto.

"You come from where? Is it really that bad?"
I don't see the horrible establishment that others speak of.
It may be I am accustomed, I may just ignore it.
But my school is fine. There are no shootings or gang fights and other evil deeds.

"They" still call it dirty, scary and dangerous, but
I'm not afraid to walk home after classes.
Though people will think it's the ghetto.
They can only think.

*Michael is a 10th grade student at Fowler High School. He enjoys watching TV, playing video games, and cooking. He is interested in pursuing acting in the future.

Syracuse

Jacqueline Perry

Growing up on Syracuse's
South Side,
Ride 'til they die
Every day someone's dying
Baby crying
Either their mother or father lying
Dead or in a heap of blood
If they make it through it will be a miracle
If they die their family will cry
And ask why
Ride 'til they die
On Syracuse's South Side

*Jacqueline is an 11th grade student at Corcoran High School.

MY HOME

Symone Sanders

Symone is a 10th grade student at Fowler High School. Her favorite activities are volunteering, reading, writing, and working with children.

My home
The 'Cuse
Not wrapped too tight
Or, in other words, loose.

Culturally diverse
So many races
But around game time
We all have orange faces.

There's always some news
Over here
Over there
Some come by two's.

We're all fans of B-ball
Some don't like us
Some may doubt us
But they come to visit our mall

But in the 'Cuse you're never alone
It's like a city on every street
This is my home

WHERE I'M FROM

Jerome Griffin

Where I'm from
Mom's seeing stars
Pop's behind bars
First of the month food stamps on the card
Still no food so everybody's got to starve
So many with unseen scars
Little kids playing in the backyard
Some dude you know in a cop car
Every building with drug dealers for hilltop guards
But now I'm doing things
That I once thought was hard
Getting grades higher than the moon and Mars
Never thought I'd have a plan
That was going to take me far

Photo credit: Corey Pringle

SCORCHING SHADE

Daviny Greene

Sarah's blood lies in the furrows
Of cotton not yet harvested

Fertilizing the earth with her sweat and tears
All the while steadily pick, pick, picking
The crop that made pigs
Kings
And people not worth more than
Pigs

John's blood lies in the pine
Planks drinking the sap that bred
Future lawyers, doctors, writers

The cotton in that field devoured
Itself, but Sarah's blood remained

Trickled down deep
Into the bowels of the earth
Nurturing the soil she once wearily trod
Preparing the earth for fruit that
Her lips would never touch

The drenched 2 x 4's
Reused to form the floor of some
Mom & Pop store

Trudged over by white kids
And finally black kids
Buying candy
Its sweetness
Overpowering the bitter aftertaste of
Hate, misery, oppression
Sitting under the tree

Roots entrenched
In the earth
Hot and red
With anger
Enraged
Over the strange fruit it was forced to bear

They sat and ate

But as the sun
Rolled across the sky
Its rays cut through the branches

And the tree
With its canopy
Spread out frowning down
On a world
Impoverished and erased
Devoid of recollection
Of its shame
Which was covered in earth

Was not able to shade them

Daviny is a student
at Syracuse university
in the African American
Studies program.

A DREAM DEFERRED?

Brandice Bell

He looked into the countless faces of hate that wanted nothing more
Than his demise
He stared
Unafraid
Into the mouths of dogs
Saliva dripping from their razor sharp teeth
And he said
I
Have
A
Dream

Marching gallantly on the hard pavement
Crushing the evil like cockroaches
Beneath the soles of his shoes
Shining black
Bouncing light back towards the sun
And he sang
We
Shall
Overcome

And in the throngs of people
Marching courageously alongside him like
Rows of corn on southern plantations
Were children
Children with dreams too

For every inch he grew in death
They grew
In height
In knowledge

In perseverance
In understanding
Yet never in complete attainment
Of his dream

The essence of the soul that flew quickly from his blood-soiled corpse
Into the heavens where it could at last find peace
Desperately searched for another body to inhabit
A kindred spirit to carry on the dream

But reality
Soon overtook it

Stripping its wings from its gossamer body
Leaving it to be plucked at in the streets by the
Vultures of tokenism and social absolutism

Behind the strong visage
Beneath the mahogany black skin
That took beatings and lashings
Yet stood still
Like a scarecrow amongst those corn stalks
Lay a man made of simple flesh and bone

Rendered dust by time and weathering
Yet the dream remains
Still seeking
Longing to find refuge within the flesh of yet another man
Or woman
Willing to carry the burden of the struggle
Able to see past what is
Into what could be
Determined to make the dream a reality

Is it you?

GENERATIONS

BY DAWN WIKTOROWICZ

Turn a comer, take a chance
Take one look back, just one quick glance
We're moving on, we're growing up
Like a dog growing from being a pup

You have a place of your own
Somewhere you can call home
A family you've raised, to shelter and to love
The kind that's tender, like a sheet-white dove

A quiet little place
A perfect place for you
A spouse that's lovable
Someone you call your boo

From now until then
Generation to generation
The world comes to life
With your family's formation

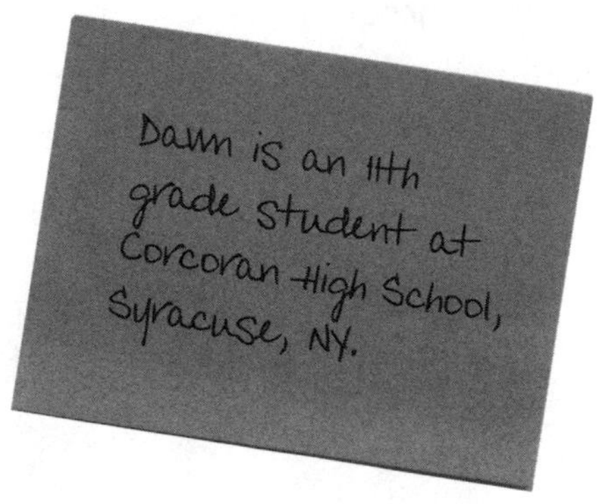

DÅ STREETS

Theresa Oakes

City—nothing like the 'burbs
streets, streets, nothing but streets.
People everywhere—
Summer is the best in the city,
people in the streets.
Playing ball, football—one hand touch or tackle.
Everyone is together, having fun,
enjoying life.
Cookouts, barbecues, beaches, pools,
bikes, cars, dogs, music, noise, noise, laughter.
But once winter comes
quiet, quiet streets, streets empty,
covered with white.
No laughter, no games,
Just streets, streets,
so white, empty.
The city in my eyes
beautiful, beautiful
When empty or full, beauty in my streets.
Beauty, beauty—in my streets.

Theresa is a 12th grade student at Fowler High School. She loves animals and aspires to be a veterinarian. She also loves basketball.

URBAN LANDSCAPE

Elizabeth Neddo

As I look out my window
what do I see?
Do I see crowded streets
full of hustlers and drug dealers?
Do I see police cars
outside my house every night?
Or do I see people sleeping under trees
because they can't afford a house?
No, that is not what I see
when I look out my window.
I see early morning runners
doing their daily exercise.
I see cars leaving their driveways
bringing their passengers to work.
I see little children
running to their bus stops.
As I look out my window
you may think I see evil things
because I live in the city
but in reality
I see people going about their lives,
doing their daily activities.

*Elizabeth is an 11th grade student at Fowler High School. She loves swimming, her friends, and being a lifeguard. She is a class officer, Jenna Foundation volunteer, and varsity swim team captain. She plans to major in athletic training in college.

COLD SILENCE

Evalena Johnson

Looking out the window
Watching the rain fall
They are watching you.
They will never speak,
They hear nothing,
They have no opinion,
And they will never judge you.
They just sit there, cold,
lifelessly watching.

*Evalena is an 11th grade student at Nottingham High School, Syracuse, NY.

WINTER

Ezekial Matos

Winter, snowy, icy
Skating, making snow angels, snowboarding
New snow, white
Ending

*Ezekiel is a 7th grade student at Blodgett Middle School. He is a first generation Syracusan. His parents were born in Puerto Rico. Zeke speaks Spanish fluently.

THE SNOW FALLS

Zoe Bonaparte

The snow falls
an inch, a foot, a mile away.
I see it fall,
as thick as a cloud
and individually.
The wind is harsh
in gusts, in bursts
and we're halfway through March.
I can't wait for sweet breezes
in April, in May,
for bright sun that brings sneezes.
For the bright spring grass
so sweet, so bright
but it will all be littered with paper and glass.
For now the blanket of snow
so clear, so bright
will not let it show.

Zoe is a 12th grade student at Fowler High School. She is Mohawk Native American. She adores her family and friends.

WHY I WRITE

BY ROBERT DANBERG

I WRITE BECAUSE OF THE RELIEF IT BRINGS ME AND THE SENSE OF WHOLENESS IT GIVES ME, BOTH WHEN I WRITE AND WHEN I FINISH SOMETHING. IT'S A FORM OF PRAYER, IN THAT I DO IT REGARDLESS OF WHAT THE OUTCOME IS AND BECAUSE NOT DOING IT WOULD BE, WELL, LONELY.

*Robert is a doctoral student and instructor in the writing Program at Syracuse university.

WHY I WRITE

BY PAT KOHLER

I WRITE TO RECALL, RELATE, REVEAL, REFLECT (MUSE), REFRESH, RESPOND, REGALE, REFUTE, REFORM, REVIVE, REJECT, RENDER, REINVENT, REJOIN, RECREATE (AMUSE), REHASH, REKINDLE, RELAX, REMARK, REMONSTRATE, REPORT, RENEGOTIATE, REPRESENT, RENEW, RENOUNCE, REPAIR, RESIST, RESERVE, REPROVE, RESTORE, RETALIATE, RESCIND, REWARD, REVIEW, REWORK, AND REVEL.

*Pat is an instructor in the writing Program at Syracuse university.

WHY I WRITE

BY DENISE VALDES-DOTY

I WRITE BECAUSE IT GIVES ME A CHANCE TO BE HEARD, ESPECIALLY ON MY BLOG. WHEN I WRITE TO FULFILL AN ASSIGNMENT, I ALWAYS TRY TO PICK A TOPIC THAT RELATES TO MY IDENTITY BECAUSE I THINK IT'S IMPORTANT TO ESTABLISH CONNECTIONS IN SPACES THAT MARGINALIZED PEOPLE HAVE BEEN EXCLUDED FROM.

*Denise is a doctoral student and instructor in the writing Program at Syracuse university. Her blog can be accessed at: http://writing.syr.edu/~dvaldesd/blog/

NATURE'S SHADOW

Katie Gaffney

When trees and plants awake in the morning,
A protecting, comforting shadow mothers all.
The birds sing a song of peaceful harmony.
The squirrels begin to go about their daily lives
Scurrying, hiding.
Life is awakening in the shadow of nature.
The trees dance in the singing breeze of the wind.
Singing, dancing, living
In perfect harmony, in the shadow of nature.
Howling wolves, running rabbits, cavorting deer.
They all know peace.

SYRACUSE SMILES

Ann Marie Taliercio

Syracuse smiles upon hearing the first notes of the cackling geese as they fly low enough to hear the swish of their wings and see the late autumn sun reflected on their bellies.

Syracuse smiles as the deer follow the seasons, always upright and proud, gracefully walking, giving a sense of renewal as the herd meets in the spring to nibble peacefully the fresh sprouts of new green life.

Syracuse smiles as the snow glistens in an early morning field on a late winter's day; as the morning doves coo, and as the road meanders through heavy-treed red apple orchards and bursting fields of yellow corn.

Syracuse smiles as the sun sinks into the lakes, smiling bright pinks, oranges and sometimes purple hues from the painted sky.

Syracuse smiles as the cows gently graze on the hills and a brilliant red cardinal allows a glimpse as it sits on a thicket's branch.

Syracuse smiles as a sacred ancient crow calls from atop the tallest pine and the hawks easily sail on the high winds above land untouched except by bare feet.

Syracuse smiles as its people are nourished by the nature that surrounds and envelopes them through time, recording stories of their lives as witnessed by the wonder of it all.

*Ann Marie is the president of UNITE-HERE Local 150 union. She resides in Syracuse, NY.

CITY SWEET SUMMER DAYS

Katie DeMong

A warm summer's day brings out the wonders of the city life with its sights, sounds, smells, and tastes. As the dawn awakens and the sun spreads its joy, the colors of summer tantalize the eyes with their pinks, reds, yellows, and vibrant greens, making the neighborhood beautiful with their elegance and grace.

As the neighbors sit on their stoop watching the pedestrians and cars drift by, young children scream with glee at the delight of visiting the Rosamond Gifford Zoo.

The pool sounds, from the city pool at Burnet,
get drowned out by the older kids' screams of laughter.
And the "Pride of the Irish" can be heard from the Blarney Stone.
As the day sets into evening, the smell of the barbecues begin
to waft into open windows and tease the stomachs of the inhabitants inside.

And when all the cooking is done, the family sits down and finally enjoys the food that their hungry, growling stomachs crave.
Chicken, macaroni salad, and potato chips satisfy the tastebuds
and complete the day of sunlight, fun, and laughter.
And as the city grows dark and the streetlights come on
one teenage girl sits on the porch enjoying the city's sweet summer days.

Photo credit: Alessia Curle

*Kathleen is a 12th grade student at Fowler High School. Some of her favorite hobbies are hanging out with friends, reading, and watching TV. The most important people in her life are her immediate family members and her best friends.

SOCIEDAD

Alexis L. Pizarro

La sociedad discrimina
No importa tus raíces
La sociedad es la que atrae
Toda la violencia que ocurre hoy en día
Si tú puedes soñar
Tú puedes lograr
No dejes que tu ambiente decida tu vida
Sé tú quien dice, "vives hoy, o mueres hoy"
Pero que seas tú y no la calle en la que vives
La calle puede escoger tu vida y que seas tú
Quien decidas
Porque solamente tú sabes lo que es mejor
Para ti.

SOCIETY

Society discriminates
It doesn't matter what
Race you are
Society is the one
That attracts all the
Violence that goes on today
If you can dream
You can do anything you want
Don't let your environment be the
One that decides your life
Let it be you who says,
"Either today I live or today I die"
But let it be you who says this and not
The street on which you live
The street can decide the outcome of your life
But don't let it do that
Be you who chooses your life
Because only you know what's best for yourself.

Aleris is a 12th grade student at Fowler High School. Her favorite activities are reading, writing, and arguing. She loves horses and dolphins.

*Photo Credit: Alfredo Del Moral

POEM TO SOCIETY

Anthony Breaker

What is it going to take?
Is it going to take niggas being extinct
before we open our eyes?
People dying in the streets
while we turn the other cheek?
Sayin' that ain't affecting me?
Well, I'll tell you right here,
we ain't gettin' nowhere.
It's time for a change.
Something different,
something cool,
something fresh,
something new.
So, I'll ask, what is it going to take?

*Anthony is a junior at Nottingham High School. He is 17 years old and a native of Syracuse, NY.

LIFE

Aleris L. Pizarro

People all around me ask
What are you doing?
And what will you be doing?
They wonder why I wish so much
and why I expect so much of life,
so I say, must it always be negative and killing?
Must I always see my peers in graves
instead of progressing in life?
Must we always attempt to kill each other
instead of trying to help one another?
Can this "ghetto," as so many call it,
be about something other than people dying,
than people suffering and only crying?
Something positive will always come out
of you and me.
If I can dream of something better,
can't you do the same?
Is it that much tougher for you to do,
or do I function differently than you?
Are we all different in the overall scheme?

LIFE

André Garrett Wilson

It is everyday life
when one wakes up in the morning to the news
and bad stories of neighborhood life.
It makes you wonder:
why is it like this, what is the violence for?
People can't get along now—the world is torn.
In every home there is a mother
who is always there for you, yet she stresses every day
wondering if you'll come home
because of the cold streets and her fear to be alone.
Every day there is a crime
every day someone is evicted, someone is convicted;
every day a child comes into this world
growing up in a home that most wouldn't call good.
The labor of this world,
the hate between boys and girls;
this is the life we live every day
in this free country we call home.

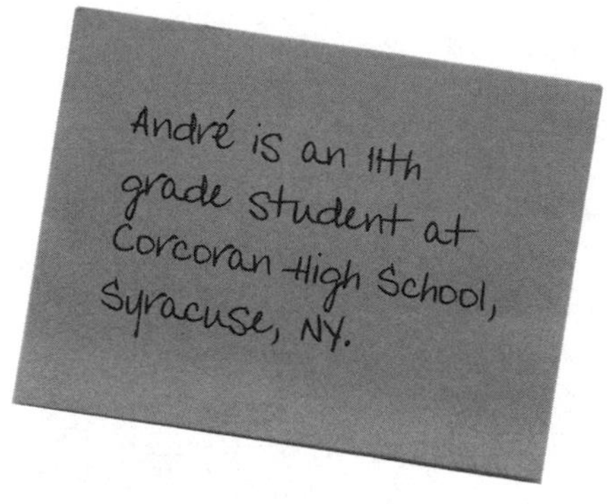

Photo credit: Courtney M. Raeford

Montel is a student at Levy Middle School, Syracuse, NY.

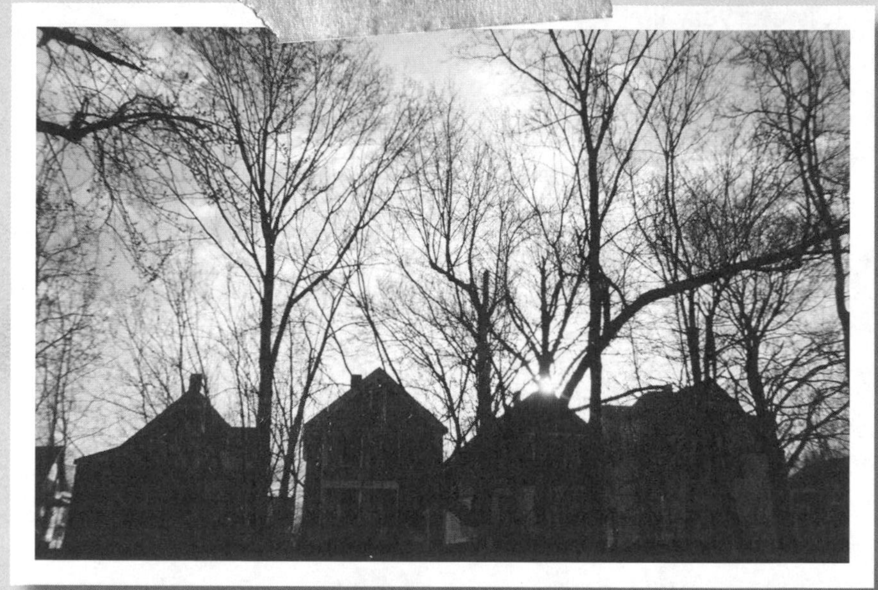

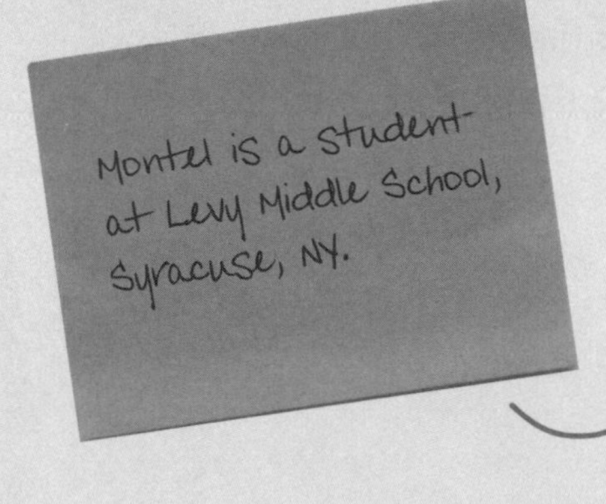

WE CAN DO ANYTHING WE SET OUR MINDS ON

Montel Webster

We can come
We can leave
We can stay
We can grieve

We can cry
We can complain
We can be happy
We can dance in rain

We can write
We can draw
We can watch
We can fall

We can smoke
We can sniff
We can be clean
We can

We can do anything we set our minds on.

DANCE YOUR HERITAGE

Lauren Ligon

Dance your heritage
Step, swing, sons of kings

Tap into your
eternal springs

Performance,
Emotions, excitement in motion
journey through time

A driving devotion
So dance to remember,
dance to forget

Celebrate your heritage,
Get lost in sweat

*Lauren is an 8th grade student at Levy Middle School. She enjoys reading, drawing, and talking to friends on the computer.

Photo credit: Courtney M. Raeford

Photo credit: Lizbeth Ramos

*Lizbeth is an 8th grade student at Shea Middle School. She is a native of Syracuse, NY. Lizbeth enjoys writing and is looking forward to having a great summer before moving on to high school in the fall.